Pedro's Pan

A Gold Rush Story

Written by Matthew Lasley

Illustrated by Jacob Souva

ALASKA
NORTHWEST
BOOKS®

He is Pedro, and I am Pan.
Up here, on Pedro's pack!

I am not a Frying Pan.
I am a Gold Pan.

You can call me Pan for short.

Pedro is a prospector. He likes looking for gold, and I help him.

Looking for gold is hard work.

It means a lot of walking and digging. There are no roads or trails out here, so we have to climb over mountains. We whack our way through thick brush. We wade through cold streams.

And I am always on the lookout for wild animals.

H₂OoSH

But it is not all work. We have fun, too.
I like hiking up the snow-peaked mountains
so we can slide back down!

PLINK PLINK PLINK CRACKLE SIZZLE POP

Pedro enjoys
berry picking.

And we both love
cooking over a campfire.

On sunny days
I shade
Pedro's eyes.

On rainy days
I keep
his head dry.

But no matter what we do, we like searching for gold most of all.

We wade through icy creeks searching for signs of gold. Pedro scoops up a small white stone.

"Quartz," he says. "This might be the place to find gold."

Pedro fills me up with gravel from the stream bank and then lowers me into the water before giving me a good shake. This settles any gold to the bottom of the pan. Then he dips me in and out of the stream, carefully washing away the dirt.

SWISH SHAKE DIP SWISH

The water is cold, but it
is the only way we can
find what we're looking for.

Look, Pedro! Is that gold?

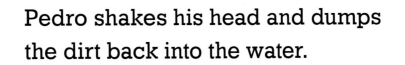

Pedro shakes his head and dumps
the dirt back into the water.

Creek after creek, we search. Pedro sifts some
fine black sand through his fingers and smiles.
"This might be the place to find gold."

He dips me in the water and fills me with gravel and dirt.

Something glints in the black sand.

Look, Pedro! I think I see gold!

SWISH SHAKE DIP SWISH

Pedro smiles and leans in real close. His smile fades and he shakes his head.

"Drat! Fool's Gold," he says, dumping the sand back into the creek.

Iron pyrite gets me every time! It is shiny like gold and fools many prospectors. But it is not what we are looking for.

We keep searching. Some days we see
other prospectors with their pans, and some
of them show off the gold they have found.

Most days we are on our own.

With each empty pan, I see the disappointment on Pedro's face.

I begin to wonder if I am broken. I am not a very good Gold Pan. Pedro probably thinks I am a Fool's Gold Pan.

Then one day, Pedro stops suddenly in the middle of the creek. It doesn't look any different from any of the other creeks that we have already checked.

"This might be the place to find gold," he says. "Look at all the rusty quartz in the creek bend."

He dips me in the water and fills me with gravel and dirt.

Again.

SWISH
SHAKE
DIP
SWISH

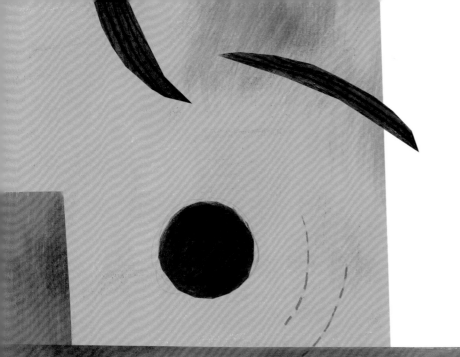

Look, Pedro! More Fool's Gold.

Pedro leans in close. Then he leans back. Then he leans in closer…

What does he see?

Pedro suddenly leaps up
and begins dancing a jig.
"Wahoo!" he shouts.

*What is it, Pedro? Do you see
a moose? Is it a bear? Did a
mosquito fly up your nose?*

Pedro hoists me into the air and we dance a jig around the creek. Cold water splashes everywhere as he yells, "We did it! We found gold!"

Pedro picks out the small nuggets of gold and puts them in a jar. Then we jump back into the creek to pan for more.

At the end of the day, we sit together next to the fire and look at all the gold we found.

It glows brightly in the firelight. I am glowing too, proud to be Pedro's Pan.

FELIX PEDRO

The Real Pedro

Pedro was inspired by a real prospector, Italian immigrant Felice Pedroni, who traveled to the wilderness of Alaska looking for gold. His mining partners called him Felix Pedro and the name stuck.

On July 22, 1902, after years of searching, Pedro finally struck gold. Rather than claiming the land for himself, he invited his friends to join him. They named two landmarks after him, Pedro Creek and Pedro's Dome. His discovery started a second gold rush and soon Fairbanks, Alaska's second largest city, grew to support the thousands who came seeking their fortune.

Every year during the third week of July, Fairbanks celebrates Pedro's discovery with a five-day celebration called Golden Days.

How to Pan for Gold

Step 1: Find a creek you think might have gold in it. The best place to look for gold is in placer deposits. There the gold gets separated from its parent rock and can be found in the gravel of the creek. Make sure you are not on someone else's land; if you are, make sure that you have their permission to pan for gold. Also be careful that the creek isn't too swift or deep.

Step 2: Fill your pan with dirt and gravel. Look for places with quartz. Gold likes to travel with this white rock.

Step 3: Put your pan of gravel under the water. Shake it from side to side to help heavier gold settle to the bottom. Pull out bigger rocks and wash them—check for gold that may be stuck on.

Step 4: Once you have only smaller gravel in the pan, repeat step 3 again.

Step 5: Tilt the pan to a 45-degree angle. Swish water over the gravel and let the lighter dirt slosh out of the pan, like waves lapping a beach.

Step 6: After you have removed about a quarter of the dirt, level the pan and shake it so the dirt settles to the bottom. Pick out bigger rocks. Tilt the pan to a 45-degree angle and tap the side to settle any gold to the lowest spot, which should be the ring at the bottom of the pan. Keep slowly removing dirt, stopping to resettle.

Step 7: When all you have left is a few tablespoons of dirt, you are ready to spot gold. Tilt the pan and tap the side. Put in just enough clean water to cover the dirt. Slowly swirl the water by rolling your wrist and causing a small wave to wash around the bottom of your pan. Go just fast enough to push dirt away. The heaviest material will move last. If you are lucky, you will spot some gold flakes in your pan!

Gold Facts

For thousands of years, cultures around the world have valued gold. People who search for gold are called prospectors. There are many ways to find gold, but in stream (or placer) deposits, a gold pan is still the best tool. Though pans have changed over the years, using one and the thrill of finding gold has not. Did you know…

1. Gold is 19 times heavier than water.

2. Gold has been discovered on every continent, even Antarctica.

3. Three Olympic-sized swimming pools would hold all the gold ever mined.

4. Scientists believe most of Earth's gold came from meteorites that crashed into the planet millions of years ago.

5. The fear of gold is called aurophobia.

6. A single ounce of gold, which is about the size of a gaming die, can be rolled out into 50 miles of wire!

7. The largest gold nugget ever found came from Australia and weighed over 173 pounds.

8. Gold never rusts.

9. An Olympic Gold medal contains only 1% gold.

10. You can eat gold!

For my dad who taught me to pan for gold.
To my wife, who is the gold of my heart.
—Matthew Lasley

To my boys, Caleb and Alex.
—Jacob Souva

MATTHEW LASLEY grew up in the interior
of Alaska, where his family mined for gold both
in Alaska, and in the Klondike. He currently
lives in Anchorage, Alaska, where he teaches
elementary students. During the summer months,
Matthew enjoys getting out along the local
streams with his friends in hopes of finding
a few flakes of gold in his pan.

JACOB SOUVA earned his BFA in Illustration
from Syracuse University. He is inspired by
Maurice Sendak, Bill Peet, and Ed Emberely,
and enjoys making kids laugh and think with
his work. Jacob lives in upstate New York
with his beautiful wife and two amazing sons.
He loves camping and hiking with them and
would like to visit Alaska one day.

Text © 2019 by Matthew Lasley
Illustrations © 2019 by Jacob Souva

Edited by Michelle McCann

Library of Congress Cataloging-in-Publication Data

Names: Lasley, Matthew, author. | Souva, Jacob, illustrator.
Title: Pedro's pan / written by Matthew Lasley ;
    illustrated by Jacob Souva.
Description: Berkeley, CA : Alaska Northwest Books, [2019] |
    Summary: Everyday is an adventure for Pedro and his Pan as
    they look for gold together in Alaska. Inspired by the true story
    of prospector Felice Pedroni and includes a brief biography,
    gold facts, and how to pan for gold. |
Identifiers: LCCN 2018014339 (print) | LCCN 2018020402 (ebook) |
    ISBN 9781513261881 (ebook) | ISBN 9781513261874 (hardcover)
Subjects: LCSH: Pedroni, Felice, 1860-1943--Fiction. | Alaska--History--
    1867-1959--Fiction. | CYAC: Pedroni, Felice, 1860-1943--Fiction. |
    Gold mines and mining--Alaska--Fiction.
Classification: LCC PZ7.1.L373 (ebook) | LCC PZ7.1.L373 Pe 2019 (print) |
    DDC [E]--dc23
LC record available at https://lccn.loc.gov/2018014339

Printed in China
22 21 20 19 1 2 3 4 5

Published by Alaska Northwest Books®
An imprint of Graphic Arts Books

GraphicArtsBooks.com

Proudly distributed by Ingram Publisher Services

GRAPHIC ARTS BOOKS
Publishing Director: Jennifer Newens
Marketing Manager: Angela Zbornik
Editor: Olivia Ngai
Design & Production: Rachel Lopez Metzger